NEMRUL

THE

PRIEST

PART 2

EXONA MOLL

urlink
PRINT & MEDIA

1603 Capitol Ave., Suite 310 Cheyenne, Wyoming USA 82001
1-888-980-6523 | admin@urlinkpublishing.com

URLink Print and Media is committed to excellence in the publishing industry.

Book design copyright © 2022 by URLink Print and Media. All rights reserved.

Published in the United States of America

Library of Congress Control Number: 2022908994
ISBN 978-1-68486-182-8 (Paperback)
ISBN 978-1-68486-183-5 (Digital)

24.05.22

PROLOGUE

The country had been wrecked by war. A few years before there had been an invasion from the north. Much of the countryside had been stripped bare. Most of the men of working age had been killed or captured. Not only had there been the main invasion, there had also been a number of later attacks that had decimated many of the farms that had survived the first wave of attacks.

Pops had inherited the small farm from his father and his father before him. He was now an old man. During the first wave of attacks, he had lost all three of his sons. He now only had his daughter Terrace and a few maids.

The farm where his nieces Arlaya and Garetta had lived had also been badly hit in the first attacks. It had also been attacked more recently by a small band of rogue soldiers, leaving them with nothing.

Within days of that attack, three priests from the temple in the city, which had been destroyed by the invaders, had sought refuge there. The sisters were about to flee to their uncle's farm, they decided to take the priests with them.

Arlaya, the older sister fell in love with the High Priest Nemroz. They soon got married and had a son, who they called Roz. Not long before their son was born, they had rescued a man they discovered in a bad way in one of the fields. When he recovered it was discovered he was one of the priests who travelled with the invaders. His name was Arken. He had been allowed to stay and was helping on the farm.

The three local priests, who were Nemroz, Polto and Darius, knew of these other priests and their beliefs from a time in the city. The local priests, led by Nemroz accepted Arken's beliefs and were about to convert to the new beliefs.

Arken had explained that to demonstrate that new believers had made a commitment to follow his God, there was a public ritual that involved each individual being dunked in water.

Arken preformed the baptisms in a stream a day's journey from the farm. Next day Nemroz returned to the farm to tend and gather the vegetables, and the rest of the group continued to take the cow to be serviced at Pop's brother's farm.

During the journey a terrible disaster befell them. A band of soldiers attacked them. They put up a fight, but their weakened group were greatly outnumbered. Polto and Darius were killed, and most of the maids were killed or captured by the soldiers. Only Arken, Terrace and one of the maids survived. They made it back to Pop's farm in a sorry state.

CHAPTER

1

They were found in the yard and fetched into the kitchen. Nemroz was distraught. He could not control himself, he rushed outside and howled. In time he came back in to help. Terrace was helped to her room. Arken and the maid were helped to the servants' quarters. Arlaya went to help Terrace, and Nemroz helped Arken to his room.

Nemroz fell at his feet sobbing. "What happened to my dear friends?"

Arken welcomed him to sit beside him. "I am dreadfully sorry. It all happened so quickly. I was trying to defend the women. It was not until it was all over that I found Polto and Darius dead. I am most dreadfully sorry."

Nemroz was too emotional to speak, he sat at Arken's feet and wept. When at last he was able to speak he sobbed, "Where are they? What have you done with their bodies?"

"We did the best we could."

"I realize we need to help you three who survived, but I must go to them. They deserve a decent burial. Are you all right for tonight? I must go to Arlaya."

"The women did all they could for now. I need to rest tonight."

"I will see you in the morning. Will you be able to get to the maids if you need help in the night?"

"I will be fine. Do not worry about me."

So Nemroz returned to the cottage. He could not face a meal, so he went straight to their room.

When it came to mealtime Arlaya was worried when Nemroz was not there, and when she went to their room she was surprised when she found he was in their bed. He had been crying. He looked up helplessly, "I suppose Roz will need feeding. I need to talk to you."

"It is alright I fed him before I came up. I only have to settle him. I will be with you shortly."

Nemroz was so relieved when Arlaya slid in beside him. "Oh my darling. Did Arken tell you…?" his voice died away. She threw her arms round him.

"They didn't give them a proper burial." He sobbed. "I must go to them."

"Darling that will not be safe."

"I should have been there to protect them."

Arlaya did not say, 'We needed you here,' because she could see how upset he was.

"I have you and that means the world to me. But what will I do without them?"

"Darling I love that you are so gentle, but it causes you such pain. Please just love me."

"I want you so much. But how could I?"

She had learnt to help him the way his dear helper from the temple had done, and gradually he responded. When they had done, they went to sleep in each other's arms. When Roz woke Arlaya fed him. Then they went down to breakfast.

When Pops came through, he said to Nemroz, "After breakfast come and see me."

Nemroz was surprised that Pops acknowledged him, but as soon as he had eaten his meagre breakfast, he came to his side.

Pops explained, "We have nothing left. We will have to leave this place. I suppose since you married my niece you will have to come too."

"Where will we go sir?"

"It will have to be my brother's farm. I only hope they still have something left."

"How will you get there sir?"

"There is no way I can walk that far. We still have a cart, but we have no animals at all now."

"If the cart is still useable, we will have to pull it by hand."

Pops looked surprised. But he said, "Get Terrace and Arken to see me."

"Sir they are both badly hurt, I will ask them."

Arlaya and Garetta her sister both came to see Pops and Nemroz went to see Arken.

"Dear Arken. Is it wrong to address you like that?"

"It is comforting to receive your friendship."

"Are you feeling any better?"

"I fear my recovery will take a while."

"Sorry I find this hard; I miss my friends so much."

"I am dreadfully sorry I was not able to protect them, please forgive me."

Nemroz sat by his bed, trying hard to control his tears. Staring at the floor he continued, "I come with a message from Pops, but I urgently wish to speak to you myself."

"Come and sit by me and tell me what troubles you."

"I should convey the message from Pops and be concerned with the matters of the farm."

"But you are more concerned about your friends."

Nemroz could hold his feelings no longer, and he broke down.

"My dear friend, I understand your grief. I feel guilty, and at least partly responsible for your loss."

"I should hate you, but I don't"

"Thankyou, please talk to me if you think it will help."

"There is so much I want to know, but it is too painful."

"Please sit by me, it would be hard for me to join you on the floor."

Emotion got the better of Nemroz, he sprang up, sank onto the bed and with his head on Arken's lap he openly wept. Touched by his distress, he sat there on the bed and held him.

Eventually Nemroz sat up saying, "Forgive me. We need to sort out what needs to be done about the farm."

"Yes later. What is it you want to know? I am dreadfully sorry I cannot tell you more details of what happened to your friends."

"There is something else." Nemroz whispered.

"I hope it is something I will be able to tell you." When Nemroz hesitated, Arken said gently, "I will tell you if I can. What is troubling you?"

"Did your Lord accept them, and is that all wasted now?"

"I am sure the Lord accepted them especially Darius, his love was very strong, and his commitment seemed very genuine."

"Does that end with death?"

"There was still much more to teach you, I had no idea time was so short. No that is not the end. The sacrifice the Lord made, was the end of death. The physical sinful body must die, but the new life that was born in all three of you when you accepted the gift from the Lord will live for ever."

"Where?"

"In your case, you are still alive. So yours still lives in your physical body."

"But Darius?"

"Darius is with the Lord."

Still a little confused Nemroz just wept.

In time he pulled himself together. "I need to ask much more about that. But at the moment we must help Pops sort out what will happen to the farm. Are you strong enough to come to the cottage? Oh forgive me. Have you had some breakfast?"

"Yes, the maids brought me some. Please help me, I will try to come to the cottage."

Every part of Arken's body hurt, but with the help of Nemroz he drew his legs over the edge of the bed and stood up. Very slowly and with several stops, they made it to the kitchen. Arlaya and Garetta had already been talking to Pops for some time. It had been decided that they would try to reach Pops's brother's farm as soon as possible. But the problem was transporting their possessions, supplies and the wounded plus Pops. Pops had told the girls there was a cart that was probably big enough. But how could it be pulled? Arken and Nemroz joined them round the table. They were surprised but pleased, that Arken had managed it.

Nemroz announced he would not be capable of pulling the cart on his own. He asked to see the cart and whether it would be possible to shift it, if everybody who was fit could help him to pull or push the cart between them. One of the maids took Nemroz to see the cart, while the others helped Pops to count up how many there were who could help.

Pops was grumbling that Arken would be another person to ride on the cart. But Garetta reminded him that Arken had been helping on the farm for some time. And when Garetta asked him straight out, he agreed that his daughter probably would not be alive if he had not been there to defend her.

Later that afternoon Nemroz agreed to try to pull the cart with help, and urgent arrangements began to be made. Over the next few days, the cart was cleaned and got in good working order. A harness was made for Nemroz to wear to help him pull the cart and everyone else would push from the sides or behind. It was sorted out what was essential for them to take and the few supplies they had were collected up.

The maids were doing their best to treat the wounds of the injured. It was several days later when everything that was to be taken was loaded on the cart and Pops, Arken, Terrace and the maid, were helped or lifted on top.

CHAPTER

2

Nemroz was strapped into the harness and everyone else pushed from the sides or from behind. After a sad good-bye the strange party started out. It was a big gamble whether or not they would be attacked again, but they had little choice.

Pops was giving instructions from his seat on the cart. Nemroz took the strain, and everyone pushed, the cart started to roll. They walked for several hours before everyone was tiring, and Pops called a halt. It was making much slower progress than it had been before.

Nemroz released himself from the harness and fell to his knees. Arlaya ran to his side.

He gasped, "Ask Pops how far it is to the stream."

The reply came back at this speed several hours yet. We will not make it by tonight."

Arlaya helped him up and he went to Pops himself.

"Just on foot, would I make it to the stream and back tonight?"

"If you can walk at a reasonable speed, you probably could."

To Arlaya Nemroz said, "Are there any maids who are strong enough to help me? If so, get them to bring some water carriers."

"Darling, you are exhausted."

"We need water. I will rest when we get back."

They had five water carriers, and four maids volunteered. Nemroz was asking for directions to the stream when one of the older maids came forward saying, "I know the way, I will come with you."

The six of them set out.

When they reached the stream, they all slaked their thirst, then filled the water carriers. Nemroz climbed the bank and called, "Come on, we must get going if we are to get back to the others by night fall." Nemroz carried one carrier, and the maids carried the rest between them.

While they were away the rest of the maids prepared some kind of a meal out of the meagre supplies they had. And others made a cover over the cart for the night.

As soon as Arlaya saw them coming, she ran to meet them, offering to help Nemroz. But he insisted she helped the maids. On reaching the cart the carriers were hung from the cart and a share of water was given out to everyone. Arlaya brought some food and some water for Nemroz.

As soon as he had finished Arlaya begged him to come and rest. She told him the family were sleeping on the cart. That the maids would find shelter in groups and that they were sleeping with Roz under the cart. Nemroz agreed, crawled under the cart, and went straight to sleep.

Next morning when he woke all his muscles hurt. Arlaya helped by massaging him, which eased them a little. He ate what little food there was. Then insisted they got started. He strapped himself into the harness, and called for everyone to push. The maids tended to take it in turns to push, but Nemroz's drive was unrelenting. But it was Pops who was shouting directions.

By the second night they had reached the stream, which helped a lot. Now they had access to water and finding their way was just a matter of following the stream. But Nemroz did not let up. He pushed on day after day.

But Arlaya was getting worried, his shoulders bled with the chafing of the harness and his feet were bleeding because his inadequate footwear did not really protect his feet. Arlaya begged him to rest, but he insisted they were in danger in the open countryside.

After many days the food rations had all but run out. Each night Nemroz had been asking Arken where he had laid his friends.

Then one evening Arken came to Nemroz saying, "I think we are nearly there now. Tomorrow we should find them."

Nemroz turned to Arken, "My dear friend, are you feeling strong enough to walk with me tomorrow?"

Arken was surprised when Nemroz addressed him as his dear friend. He had always felt so guilty that he had not been able to save Darius.

"Nemroz we have been saying for days you should have help."

"It is not help pulling I am asking for. I want you to guide me to Darius."

"My dear, dear friend. Can you cope with that?"

"Darius deserves a decent burial. I intend to give him one."

The next day Arken, Arlaya and Garetta insisted on helping Nemroz. Nemroz was strapped into the harness, in spite of the state he was in. Arken took the weight of one shaft, and the sisters together took the weight of the other. And Nemroz pulled and guided the cart. No one had realized until then that Nemroz had been secretly crying with the pain.

It was into the afternoon when Arken stopped and cried out, "They are down there."

"Arken please help me with the straps. Will you be able to come with me?"

Pops was shouting, "Why have we stopped?"

Most of them knew what Nemroz was doing. And they took no notice of Pops.

Arken and Nemroz helped each other down the bank. Several others followed. Nemroz began digging at the small mounds by the water's edge. The first he found was Polto's jet black hair.

He turned to Arken saying, "Please can you…" then Nemroz started on the next mound. Frantically digging with his bare hands. When a partly decomposed body started to appear, he gently continued removing the dirt, completely oblivious of anyone else. Slowly Darius's remains were revealed. Nemroz had tied the makeshift shroud he had brought around his waist. He laid it on the ground and begged Arken to help. The tears were streaming down Nemroz's face as he and Arken carefully lifted the remains onto the shroud. Nemroz gently wrapped what was left of the body and secured the shroud. Then he cried, "How will we get him to the cart?"

Oblivious of the state of their own bodies, they managed to get the shrouded body to the cart.

It was not until then that Nemroz realized just how much every part of his body hurt.

They found that Pops had sent some of the maids on ahead to ask for help from his brother.

They turned round and the others who had followed them down to the stream had managed to rescue Polto's body, and they were struggling to carry it up the bank.

Nemroz cried, "Wait I have something for a shroud." He struggled onto the cart and fetched another length of cloth, which he passed to Arken. He gazed down helplessly at Darius's shrouded body saying desperately, "At the moment I can't even lift Darius, let alone Polto."

Arken replied, "We will do it between us, no one is expecting you to do it. Please come down."

Pops was furious, he said, "I am not having corpses on my cart with me."

Arken helped the maids bring Polto's remains to the top of the bank. Then he and Nemroz wrapped him in the makeshift shroud. For the time being they laid both of them beneath the cart. By then it was evening, Arlaya begged Nemroz to come and rest. Exhausted, bleeding and in pain, he crawled under the cart, weakly held out his arms to Arlaya. Then just fell asleep.

The next morning Pops called (what he still called the family). But he still insisted that Nemroz was not family, to discuss what to do next. Arlaya shouted, "Nemroz has been pulling the cart all this time, he should be here."

Pops snorted, "If he doesn't want to do it anymore, we'll wait for my brother."

"But Pops we have no food left."

"If your precious Nemroz was any good he could catch something."

Nemroz could hear what was being said from where he lay. He wept. He gazed at the shrouds, and he so wished he could run to Darius.

"Pops we need to know whether he can go any further."

"I told him to go ages ago. I never wanted those troublesome priests around in the first place."

"Without my 'troublesome priest' we would not be here. We would not be able to push the cart without him."

"We managed before they came on the scene."

"You pull the cart then." Arlaya shouted and left.

She leapt off the cart and was so relieved that Nemroz was still there. She rushed into his arms.

"Before when he told you to go, you just went on working."

"What do you want me to do?"

"Are you going to do that again?"

"Pops will not have what is left of my dear friends on the cart. I am not leaving without them."

"Oh Nemroz, I have always felt I have shared you with those priests of yours."

"Would you have me leave them?"

"This means a lot to you, doesn't it?"

"You know it does."

"If I could get Pops to have them on the cart. Would you pull it again?"

"If we stay here, if the help from Pops's brother doesn't come, we will starve."

"Please come with me to see Pops."

"He would not see me."

"He is no longer strong enough to throw you off. I want him to see you."

Reluctantly he followed Arlaya, and she helped him on the cart.

"What are you doing here."

Arlaya stepped in, "I asked him to come. I want you to see what he has done for us."

To Nemroz's horror, she ripped off his shirt. Everyone gasped at the state of his shoulders. Pops was about to deride him, but then he stopped.

With a look of embarrassment Nemroz took his shirt and put it back on.

Then Arlaya asked, "Are you prepared to pull the cart until we meet the team from the farm?"

"If your uncle is prepared to take what is left of my friends with us."

Pops grunted, "Get in the harness then."

Some of the maids fetched some water, everyone else helped put the shrouded bodies on the cart and Nemroz allowed himself to be strapped back in the harness. He took the strain and called, "Push!"

They trudged on for the rest of the day. Some of the maids brought water from time to time. But there was no food left. When at last they stopped Nemroz was exhausted. He crawled under the cart and in spite of the pain, fell straight to sleep.

Arlaya was really worried. Not only was she worried about Nemroz, due to the lack of food her milk was drying up and Roz was always crying.

The next day there was still no sign of the team from the farm and Nemroz was still asleep. Roz was crying and Arlaya tried to feed him.

Nemroz looked at her sleepily and said forlornly, "I wish you could feed ME."

"Nemroz darling, I can't even feed Roz."

"What do you mean?"

"There is not enough food for me to make the milk."

Nemroz did his best to jump up, "I will call the others. We must get you to this farm." He rounded up the others who were struggling as much as he was. He fetched the infant and laid him on the cart. He begged Arken to help him with the harness. Although Arken was still suffering from his own injuries, he, Arlaya and Garetta insisted on helping with the shafts. Nemroz had difficulty concealing the cry as he took the strain and called, "Push."

As the afternoon wore on Arlaya was worried they would not be able to keep going much longer. They were all struggling. They were all trudging along, hardly aware of where they were going.

Then suddenly there were excited cries up ahead, and there were some of their maids running towards them. It was Garetta who realised what was happening.

She cried out, "It's the maids, they have come with help from the farm."

Nemroz stopped, with as much disbelief as relief, he turned to Arken and begged, "Please release me."

Though Arken was hardly conscious he released the straps and Nemroz sank to his knees.

Soon the rest of the team had arrived. With the maids was a cart pulled by a cart horse, led by a man on another horse.

Arlaya fell before one of the maids asking, "Have you brought help?"

"We have food for you for now, and a cart to take you back to the farm."

On hearing this Nemroz fell at her feet pleading, "Please bring food for Arlaya and the other women."

There were the four maids who had walked the last few miles from the group to the farm. They hurriedly prepared some food for the bedraggled group. It was Nemroz himself who was helping the maids distribute the food before he collapsed. Arken and Arlaya helped him to eat.

They camped where they were for that night. Next day Pops said everything was to be transferred to his brother's cart. But when they came to the shrouded bodies he shouted, "No not them."

Arlaya looked with horror, fearing what Nemroz's reaction would be.

Gathering the little strength he had left, Nemroz came to challenge Pops, "Even if you have no respect for me, can you not have some respect for the dead?"

Pops called for the young men who came from his brother's farm. Ignoring Nemroz he said to the young men, "Get rid of these priests, all three of them."

Arlaya screamed, "No you can't do that!"

Nearly all the group surrounded the young men to support Nemroz.

Quite overcome by the show of support, Nemroz retreated under the cart and Arlaya lay by his side. All the maids gathered round them and stayed all night. Only Garetta and Terrace stayed on the cart to keep an eye on Pops. And Arken guarded the shrouded bodies.

When he woke next morning Nemroz turned to Arlaya and with a desperate tone in his voice said. "What am I to do?"

Arlaya replied sleepily, "Are they worth it?"

Which brought him to with a start, "Of course they are worth it. I thought you would support me."

"I am sorry darling. I will go and see if there is any breakfast."

The maids were beginning to wake. A few of them came and knelt by Nemroz, and said, "Just to let you know we are on your side. We think Pops is being very mean to you."

"Thankyou!"

Arlaya returned saying, "The maids are bringing some."

But by then Roz was weakly crying. Arlaya fetched him, but he was just lying in her arms feebly crying. Nemroz reached over and gently helped him to Arlaya's breast and held them together until he took what little milk there was. When the maids came with the breakfasts, they were amazed to see what Nemroz was doing. They had never seen a man doing anything like that.

When Roz had finished Nemroz took him in his arms and encouraged Arlaya to eat the food the maids had brought.

There were voices from above, Arlaya passed Roz to one of the maids saying, "You eat your food. I will go and see what is happening."

When Nemroz heard Arlaya screaming, "You can't do that!" he realized what was happening and he went almost hysterical. He started throwing everything and everybody off the cart. Even the young men from the farm backed off. Arken had to restrain him from throwing

Pops off the cart. Pops was so stunned and shocked, he did not resist when the girls helped him down.

When Nemroz's fury was spent, he collapsed almost on top of his dead friends. When Arlaya came to him he sobbed, "I should not have left them before, I will not leave them now. Ask Arken to come to me."

"I am here dear friend."

"Please strap me in the harness. I will take them with me myself."

"You are not strong enough. Your loyalty has always amazed me, but you cannot do this."

Arlaya begged him, "There must be another way, you will kill yourself."

He gazed at her and said, "I do love you, and I thank you. You have given me more happiness than any priest should ever have."

"Darling do you not care what happens to me, and Roz needs you."

He turned to Arken and pleaded, "Please help me."

"You cannot walk from here to the farm in the state you are in, let alone pull the cart. We must find another way."

Pops had been helped onto the other cart, and was shouting about everyone should be on the cart or be left behind. Arlaya ignored him and went straight to the young men. She explained they did not want to leave Pops's cart behind. Was there any way it could be attached?"

Eventually between them they managed to attach Pops's cart behind the farm cart, with Nemroz and his friends' remains still on it. Nemroz refused to move. So Arlaya joined him with little Roz in her arms. Everyone else was on the main cart, and the strange party started off.

At last, Nemroz could rest. And as long as Pops left him alone, he left him in charge. Exhausted and battered, he was glad to hand over the reins, metaphorically and physically.

Arlaya did her best to heal Nemroz's injuries. With her care, and with food and rest he was recovering.

With two carts, one loaded with goods and people, the journey back to the farm was much slower than the outward journey, with frequent rest stops for the horses.

Nemroz sheltered his precious cargo the best he could. Arlaya knew better than to complain. Nemroz complained that it was to public on the top of the cart to be intimate, (he never fully got over the idea that he was a priest and should not have a woman).

One night the young men told Pops that they should be in the yard by the next day. They tried to limit the number of times they stopped for the horses. By mid-day they arrived in the farm. Suddenly Nemroz was worried about his situation.

He gripped Arlaya whispering, "Will Pops try to have us destroyed again?"

She tried to reassure him that they would protect him. But Nemroz lay there trembling.

Garetta and Terrace were helping Pops down from the cart.

Arlaya said to Nemroz, "I must go with them. Arken will stay with you."

The experience since they left Pops's farm had left Nemroz feeling weak and vulnerable. He was glad he had found a friend in Arken and he looked to him for comfort.

"What do you think will happen to us?"

"Did you mean your commitment that you made to my God?"

A little surprised he replied, "Yes."

"Then we will pray for comfort and reassurance."

"I still have so much to learn. Please stay with me."

"Your company is a comfort to me too, but I am worried that I will come between you and Arlaya."

"It is my desire that Arlaya will also come to know your god."

"My dear friend, you are a better evangelist than I am."

"What is an evangelist?"

"Someone who leads people to the Lord."

CHAPTER

3

Arlaya came running back, "They are saying you cannot stay. We managed to persuade them not to kill you as you are Roz's father. But we must leave now."

Nemroz panicked.

Arken calmly said, "Are the maids still in the cart?"

"I think so."

"Come we will talk with them first."

Arlaya went to protest, but Arken had already climbed down. So Arlaya and Nemroz followed.

By the time they were sitting with the maids on the other cart Arlaya had calmed down a bit.

"Now, what was actually said?" Arken calmly asked.

Pops was adamant that all the priests, alive or dead must go. He wanted them all destroyed. Even his brother said he was being unreasonable. It was agreed we could have Pops's old cart, but that we should leave the farm."

They took the covers that had been used to make a tent over the cart, and what was left of the food the young men had brought. And the few tools they could find. They discussed with the maids where they should go. The maid who had been to the farm with the family in the past said she would help. Several of the other maids said they would help push the cart.

They detached Pops's cart and Nemroz was strapped into the harness once more.

He took a deep breath and called, "Push." And off they went.

Their guide told them of a sheltered spot not far from the farm, that would be out of sight from the farm itself. It was hard going with the cart across the fields, but the cart was lighter now. They found a high hedge obscuring the view from the farm, and placed the cart on the other side of it. It was arranged where they could meet up next day and the maids left.

"Well, it could be worse." Said Arlaya, trying to sound positive. "We survived on the journey. But we will need a better shelter by the winter. I will prepare something to eat. We will make a shelter out of this in the morning."

As soon as they had eaten and Roz was fed, Arken said, "I will leave you in peace." And climbed onto the cart.

Nemroz looked longingly at Arlaya, then said, "I am sorry I have not been able to touch you for days."

Arlaya lay down and held out her arms to him. "I want you so much."

The next morning Arlaya was not happy when Nemroz insisted that the first and most important thing was to give his friends a decent burial. Not far from behind the cart Nemroz and Arken started digging a suitable hole. They fetched the two shrouded bodies, one at a time. Nemroz insisted they were lain together as they would have lain in life. Arken was not pleased with the way Nemroz was handling the burial. But realizing it was unreasonable to expect Nemroz to follow his customs yet. They very gently replace the soil. Nemroz completed his ritual with two small piles of stones. He prostrated himself on the grave and wept.

He rose and without saying another word, went in their space under the cart to see how Arlaya and little Roz were. It had been arranged for them to meet some of the maids in the evening, and Arlaya wanted to know whether to try to make another meal with the food they had, or wait to see what the maids had been able to bring. They decided to eat straight away, so Arlaya went ahead.

Later Nemroz and Arken went together to meet the maids. They had brought some stew, some milk and some fruit. They said they would bring what they could each day, but it would vary. Arken thanked the maids very much and asked whether they were in danger bringing them food.

"We will have to see. No one complained today."

It was decided to keep that food to eat next day. Arken managed as he was for another night, and Nemroz and Arlaya were together under the cart.

The next day a shelter was erected over the cart, hanging down halfway across making a door. The cover hung down to the ground at the end, making a door for the area below the cart. Then they started erecting a wall the length of the cart on the other side to the hedge and the other end. They made the walls by driving long sticks in the ground with the tops against the cart. Then weaving whatever they could find through the sticks to make a thatch. For the time being it would be adequate. So, they would have their own little home.

The next day while the men worked, Arlaya went in search of wild herbs etc. to make a treatment for Nemroz's shoulders that were still sore from the chaffing of the harness. She did find a few. She asked Nemroz if it would be safe to light a fire. It was decided they should ask the maids what the attitude towards them was first.

While Arlaya was away Nemroz and Arken were talking about the many things Arken still wanted to teach Nemroz about his God. "I am sad we did not have chance to get further with Darius and Polto."

"I know, I am very sorry about that. I have always worried you blame me for that."

"Not really. I should have been there for them."

"You cannot blame yourself, Arlaya and Roz needed you more. We must be grateful they found the Lord before they died."

"What difference will that make?"

"All the difference in the world. I had not had chance to explain properly. When we are born as a baby, that is our physical birth. That life dies when we die. But when we come to accept the Lord, a spirit is born in us. That spirit lives for ever. Our spirit is released at the death of our physical body, then our spirit goes to be with the Lord. Can you understand that?"

"I will have to think about it. Does all this apply the same for my friends?"

While Nemroz was still thinking about it, Arlaya returned. When she was told she could not have a fire straight away, she was unhappy she would have to wait to make the treatment. She just said, "It is you that hurts not me. And we will have to eat cold stew."

Soon after they had eaten the stew, Nemroz and Arken were about to leave to meet up with the maids, when Arlaya stated she wanted to come too.

Nemroz asked, "Who will look after Roz?"

"I want to ask about lighting fires."

"Do you not trust me to ask? You always used to trust me about everything."

"You seem different these days."

"Please don't think I am less trustworthy. I will sort out about your fire. I will see you later. You put Roz to bed."

Arken and Nemroz left.

The maids had brought them food as before. They exchanged stew pots. Then Nemroz asked what the attitude of the family was towards them now.

The maids said, "They seem to have forgotten about you now."

"Do you think if we light a fire they will come to investigate?"

"I wouldn't imagine they would. Anyway, the farmhands aren't bothered."

They thanked the maids and left. When they got back Nemroz just said, "It will be fine to light a fire." And went to bed.

The next morning as Arlaya was preparing some breakfast she said, "After breakfast can you light a fire?"

"I am sorry darling I don't know how."

Without thinking she replied, "Did your parents not teach you anything?"

He turned away and murmured, "I never knew my parents."

"Oh my darling, I'm sorry I never thought."

When Arken came down for breakfast, Arlaya was in tears with her arms round Nemroz.

"What is wrong?"

At first Arlaya tried to shrug it off, but Nemroz said, "It's my fault, I don't know how to light a fire."

"That's okay. While I was with the army, I saw the soldiers doing that. I never did that myself, but I can try. Let's have some breakfast, then we will have a go."

Trying to fight back the tears Nemroz whispered, "I am so glad you are here."

Arlaya just grunted "Priests!" and continued with the breakfast.

After they had eaten Arken said, "Come along we will see if we can light a fire. We will all go and see what wood we can find. Roz can come along; he is trying to walk now."

They collected plenty of wood, big pieces and thin pieces. Around the cart there was dry grass etc.

Arken cleared an area for safety. Then he proceeded to try to copy what he had seen the soldiers do. He found it was harder than he thought, but eventually he succeeded. Nemroz had fetched some water and Arlaya had washed out the stew pot.

She boiled down some of the herbs to make a treatment. When it had cooled, she took Nemroz inside and removed his shirt.

"Darling I hope this works, your shoulders still look so sore."

Nemroz could not resist saying, "There may be a lot of things I don't know, but I can replace a horse."

"My darling, you are worth a lot more than that."

"I am glad you think so."

"Ask Arken to come in, I think some of his injuries are still painful."

At first Arken resisted, but Nemroz persuaded him to let Arlaya help.

Before they went back out, he also persuaded him to tell Arlaya about his god. At first, she did not want to know, but Nemroz insisted it was important. To start with she only listened to please Nemroz. But in time she became more and more interested. But her lessons were always interrupted by Roz needing attention, or him needing to be fed.

Later when it came to the meal, they were able to heat the stew. After Nemroz and Arken got back from seeing the maids they were beginning to realize they were going to have to find ways of producing food for themselves.

Nemroz said, "We cannot rely on the maids fetching food for us for ever. Tomorrow we must discuss it."

They left it at that and went to bed.

Next morning over breakfast Nemroz asked whether the other two had thought about what they should do next.

Arlaya said they should ask the maids for advice. Nemroz said they should be independent, and Arken did not really know, but Arlaya's idea seemed worth pursuing. So reluctantly Nemroz agreed. So that evening Arken asked the maids. The older maid who usually took the lead said, "Leave it with me, I will see what we can do."

The maids had been regularly bringing milk now, so Arlaya had begun supplementing Roz's milk with milksop.

Several evenings later the leading maid said, "We have had a meeting."

Nemroz drew back, but Arken held his arm.

She continued, "Most of the people there were sympathetic."

"Was Pops there?" Nemroz cut in anxiously.

"No, but his brother was. He has offered to lend you some land. And a young man offered to help. He and his wife agreed to come and stay with you if you would like that."

Nemroz gasped and turned away.

But Arken said, "That is kind. I think he should come to discuss things with us first."

"I will arrange it, and let you know tomorrow."

Nemroz took the food and hurriedly left.

As soon as they were out of earshot Nemroz exploded, "How dare you!"

Arken calmly replied, "It is my life too you know. Pops had included all priests."

"You should have discussed it with Arlaya and me."

Arken walked on in silence.

By the time they got back to the shelter Nemroz had calmed down. And he waited to see what would happen. Next day he fetched some water and collected wood. But there was not much else he could do.

He said to Arken. "At first at the farm everyone seemed to ask to much of me, I never seemed to have time to be with Arlaya. Now I have nothing to do, that seems to be even worse."

The next day, halfway through the afternoon the young couple arrived. Nemroz was shocked they knew where the three of them lived. Arken greeted them and asked them in. The young man introduced himself as Ker and said, "This is my wife Hella."

Arken replied, "You probably know who we are."

"We do sir."

"What are you offering to do?"

"We understand you know very little about farming. We were hoping to move to a farm of our own, so were glad to accept the boss's offer."

"Which is?" Nemroz cut in.

"We farm some of the land rent free if we teach you how to farm it."

Nemroz was about to but in, when Arlaya asked, "Where will you live?"

"With you to start with, if that is alright with you."

Arlaya and Arken stopped Nemroz from refusing.

Arken said, "We will give it a try. You have my quarters for now."

"Hold on I haven't agreed. And where will you go?"

Ker answered for him, "That is very kind sir. We will build a shelter for you."

"Please call me Arken." He looked expectantly at the other two, but they did not respond.

CHAPTER

4

The next day the couple returned with their few belongings. Arken showed them to what had been his quarters.

"You are very kind. Where can we build your shelter?"

"That would be appreciated,"

Ker left Hella to arrange their few things and Ker followed Arken down and round to the back wall under the cart.

"I thought we could use the end wall of Nemroz's shelter for one wall and the hedge for the other. Then a diagonal wall across the corner, with a space for an entrance."

"Will that be sufficient for you?"

"That will be fine. It is only for me."

They proceeded to gather the sticks etc. and built Arken his shelter. Arlaya prepared extra things for the meal, and they shared the stew between them. When they came in to eat, Arken asked Nemroz why he hadn't come to help.

He answered, "I am not happy with this arrangement."

Arlaya responded, "Why not?"

Nemroz looked away, then walked out.

"Nemroz, you haven't finished your meal."

Roz was settled for the night, and Arlaya was not able to sleep. Eventually Nemroz returned and lay quietly beside her.

"My darling, where have you been? What is the matter?"

He turned away whispering, "You have betrayed me into the hands of people who work for Pops. He wants to kill me."

"Oh Nemroz, Ker and Hella are here to help."

"How can you be so sure?"

"Please believe Arken, he trusts them. Please come to me."

Next day at breakfast Arlaya inquired whether Ker and Hella had been comfortable in the cart.

"Arken is kind to let us use his quarters. I hope he will be alright in his new little shelter."

"I am fine thankyou."

Ker explained they were to use the field that the cart was in and a small strip of the next field. The smaller strip is for vegetables, and the larger field is for livestock.

"There you are." Arlaya whispered to Nemroz.

"We will start on the vegetable strip today, if that is alright with both of you."

"Come on Nemroz. What is the matter with you?" Then to Ker he said, "I don't believe they introduced themselves yesterday, these are Nemroz and Arlaya. This is their little son Roz."

Ker responded with, "I hope we will get on. I am looking forward to working with you. I have heard a lot about you."

Nemroz gave him a very suspicious look.

"What tools were you given?"

Arken replied, "A spade and an axe."

"We will have to fetch some more. I was told we could borrow what we need."

When Arken and Ker went out into the field Arlaya said to Nemroz, "I am sure you are wrong about Ker. He seems a friendly young man."

"I hope you are right."

Arken said, "I wish we could get Nemroz to co-operate, I think you will find he knows quite a lot about the vegetables. He worked in the field much longer than I did. He was teaching me."

"Perhaps we could try again. It would be more helpful if he could start with the tools we have, and we could collect more. What can I do to get him to trust me?"

"He thinks you work for Pops, (as we all call Arlaya's uncle). And Pops wanted to kill him."

"I must convince him that is wrong."

They turned back to the shelter.

On entering under the cart Nemroz was still there with the women. Hella was trying to convince Nemroz that she and Ker meant him no harm. They wanted to be friends and work together. As the others entered, she was saying, "Please give us chance to show you."

Both Arlaya and Arken said, "We cannot do this on our own. Please give Ker and Hella chance to prove they mean us no harm."

Unwillingly Nemroz said he would give it a try. Arken said, "Ker has been showing me the field where we can grow vegetables. You were showing me how to prepare the ground for vegetables. Please come and help us." He turned to Arlaya and she added, "Please darling you know how."

He muttered, "No one is on my side."

"We all are. We all love you."

Then Nemroz gave in, and said, "Show me the tools and the field. I can only die once."

"No one here will kill you. We need your help."

They returned to the field and Ker showed him the section they were to use and gave him the tools. Then he left with Arken to fetch more tools.

Later they returned, Nemroz was still working away. Ker said, "I am sorry they will only allow us to have tools like spades, so it will be slow work."

"That is all I had on Pops's farm, so I am used to that."

"You have made a good start."

"I maybe was brought up as a priest, but I am capable of working."

"So I can see. Come back to the shelter for now. You need a rest."

Arken said, "You should have seen him when he was pulling the cart."

"I have heard about that."

Nemroz looked away quite embarrassed.

When they got back to the cart the women were preparing the evening meal.

Nemroz was greeted with, "Have you been alright?"

"It is good to be working again. Working in the field is better than pulling a cart."

After the meal Arken asked who was coming to collect the food, saying, "We will still need food from the maids for now."

Ker replied, "I will go with Arken if you like. Nemroz has been doing most of the work."

Nemroz did not object, so that is what they did. And Hella went to their quarters. As soon as they were alone Arlaya said, "Hella is nice. She is pregnant. It will be nice to have a friend."

Nemroz replied, "You be careful. I don't trust them"

"I don't know what is the matter with you lately. You won't go like Polto, will you?"

Nemroz looked away very hurt, and went to bed. Not waiting for Arken and Ker to return.

When the other three came for breakfast next day, Arken said, "Are we all going to work in the field today?"

"Someone needs to." Nemroz replied.

Ker said, "I asked the maids to ask for some seeds for us to sow. We need to have the ground ready."

Arlaya cut in, "Nemroz I have not treated your shoulders yet this morning."

"Don't worry they are alright."

"Come on no one will mind waiting." She removed his shirt and proceeded to dress the wounds. Ker and Hella gasped,

"That is what happened when he was pulling the cart. Pops says he is useless. He nearly killed himself trying to get us to safety."

Ker said, "It seems the stories about you are not exaggerated. I am honoured to be working with you."

"Go on I'm not that good."

They collected the tools and set out for the field again.

Ker said, "I think we should work a patch each."

They worked several hours, then Ker and Arken wanted a break. Nemroz was still working. Ker came and said, "Come and have a break with us."

"The work won't get done by sitting about."

"Come I want to talk to you."

"What about?"

"Come and find out."

"Alright."

"I was fascinated by the tales the maids were telling us about you."

"Why would they tell tales about ME?"

"It sounds as though the tales about you pulling the cart were true."

"What else were they saying about me?"

"I hope this will not upset you, but they said about your loyalty to your friends."

Nemroz turned away saying, "Did they?"

Arken looked worried as Ker continued, "Did you bring them here?"

Nemroz moaned, "I told Arlaya you are from Pops."

"Believe me I am not. If they are friends of yours, they are friends of mine. I wish to show them my respects."

"What, so you can dig them up and destroy them"

"That is unkind. I care about your loss."

Arken was getting uncomfortable and returned to work.

"Nemroz please, let us be friends."

"You can kill me, but don't harm my friends."

"Please let me show you I wish to be friends. Let me show respect to your friends."

Reluctantly Nemroz stood and took Ker by the hand. He walked in silence to his friends' grave. Ker prostrated himself on the grave. Nemroz knelt by Darius with his head on his cairn.

Arken worked on for a while. Then he collected up the tools and returned to the shelter. By then Nemroz and Ker had re-joined the women. It was the first time for a long time Arken had felt a foreigner in a foreign land. He crawled into his little shelter and knelt quietly praying.

It was nearly time for their meal and Arken still had not re-joined the others. Nemroz thought he was still in the field, but he found the tools lying by the outer wall.

He called, "Arken where are you? Are you alright?"

His voice was getting more anxious, so Arken crawled out.

"Oh, there you are. Are you unwell?"

"You have people from your own land again now."

Without thinking Nemroz threw his arms round him, "My dear friend, we still want you."

Arken suddenly found the embrace reassuring, and tears came unbidden to his eyes. He through his arms round Nemroz and Nemroz nearly kissed him.

"Come it's mealtime. You are one of us now." He said brushing a tear from Arken's cheek.

After they had eaten Nemroz and Ker went to meet the maids, while Arlaya and Hella sat talking to Arken.

Next morning Ker and Hella came for breakfast, but Arken was nowhere to be seen. Nemroz went looking for him. He called outside his little shelter, but he did not answer. When he looked inside Arken's little shelter, he was lying face down.

"What is the matter? Are you ill?"

Arken looked up. "No, I have just realized I am a poor priest. I have deserted my beliefs and failed my Lord."

"Why what have you done?"

"When we were working at the farm, I told you I was to dedicate one day in seven to my Lord. Since we left the farm, I have not done that once. What kind of example is that to you? I was praying to my Lord for forgiveness."

Nemroz looked concerned, "Will he forgive you?"

"If we are truly sorry, He has promised always to forgive us. I will fast for today to show I mean it. Will you join me later? We can pray together, and I will teach you more of what you need to know."

"Does this seventh day rule apply to me?"

"As you made a commitment to the Lord, yes it does."

"It is rather cramped in your little shelter. Can we meet by the grave?" Arken hesitated. "Polto and Darius made a commitment too."

So Arken agreed.

While eating breakfast Nemroz explained he would be with Arken for the rest of the day and said, "In Arken's religion he needed to dedicate one day in seven to his god. And since I have made a commitment to Arken's god, I need to join him. If any of you want to join us, you are welcome."

Arlaya hesitated, but when Hella did not want to know, she said, "No."

Ker was annoyed, "The maids brought us seeds yesterday. They need sowing. It sounds as though I will be working on my own. I did not think you were like that Nemroz."

CHAPTER

5

Nemroz arrived at the graveside first. He prostrated himself on the grave until Arken arrived, when he rose and knelt by the cairn to Darius and Arken joined him.

Arken said, "I want you to learn how we do things." But he did not challenge his approach to the grave. "We start by offering the gathering to the Lord and asking Him to join us."

Nemroz looked puzzled, but he did not comment, he just said, "I asked the others to come, but they did not want to know."

"You looked puzzled by what I said. I have told you that God wants a relationship with mankind. We know Him through our spirit. First we need to ask for forgiveness for anything we have done wrong."

"I don't think I have done anything wrong."

"Unfortunately, we are not capable of living a perfect life, so we will always be in need of forgiveness. So we will pray."

"I do not know how to pray"

"Nor did the Lord's first followers, so he taught them this standard prayer.

Our Father who art in heaven, hallowed be Thy name.

Thy kingdom come, Thy will be done on earth as it is in heaven.

Give us this day our daily bread.

Forgive us our trespasses. As we forgive others who trespass against us.

Lead us not into temptation, but deliver us from the evil one."

"Hold on I do not understand a lot of that."

"Alright, I will go through it a bit at a time.

"'Our Father' Our Lord taught us to look to God as a father.

'Who art in heaven' Heaven is where we think of as where God is.

'Hallow be Thy name' Hallow is to honour and hold as holy.

'Your kingdom come'

I don't think you have a king, he is the supreme leader, so a kingdom is what he rules.

'Your will be done' Is asking for our world to be run by God's rules.

'Give us this day our daily bread' Is asking for God's provision.

'Forgive us our trespasses (wrongdoings), as we forgive those who trespass against us'

Means we must forgive others as we wish to be forgiven.

'Lead us not into temptation' I think you know what temptation is.

'Deliver us from the evil one'

The evil one, is our spiritual enemy who tries to keep us from knowing God.

Does that help? I do not expect you to remember all of that straight away."

"It will not take me long to learn that."

"There is something else I want you to master."

"What is that?"

"I want you to talk quietly threw your spirit to the Lord. I would not expect everyone to do that yet. But I think you will be able to do that."

"Do you think I have a spirit?"

"I explained that your spirit was born in you when you accepted the Lord and made the commitment. Do you believe that?"

Nemroz hesitated, then said, "I am not sure."

"I am not going to push you. But I am going to stay quiet the rest of the day. I need to re-establish my commitment to the Lord."

"Can I show respect to my friends at the same time?"

"If you feel more comfortable. But remember it is your commitment to the Lord that is the most important."

Arken knelt by the hedge and Nemroz prostrated himself on the grave. It was late afternoon when Nemroz asked if Arken was coming for the meal.

Arken said, "I am fasting until tomorrow. You go ahead."

And without saying anymore, Nemroz left.

When he got back the women were busy outside the shelter. Roz tottered up to meet him, but the greeting from the women was not so friendly. A little upset Nemroz said, "What is the matter?"

Arlaya said, "Why didn't you help Ker?"

"I thought you were interested in what Arken was doing."

"The seeds needed sowing."

"One day would not make much difference."

Hella interrupted, "Ker didn't think so."

"I will be helping tomorrow."

"Oh will you?"

Thinking saying anymore would not help, he went inside the shelter, wishing Arken was there. Roz followed him, so he sat playing with him until the food was ready.

By then Ker had returned from the field saying, "Where are those lazy priests?"

Newroz emerged, "You know that is not true. Far be it for me to boast, but who dug a lot of the field and what of the tales of me and the cart."

Arlaya looked shocked and through her arms around his wounded shoulders, "All right you two, come and have your food. Where is Arken?"

"He will not be eating until tomorrow."

Everyone ate in silence.

Later Nemroz said, "As Arken is not here this evening, I will come with you to fetch the food from the maids."

Ker did not answer. They walked together in silence.

Later when everyone had settled and Nemroz lay with Arlaya,

He said, "Why did you turn on my? Don't you love me anymore?"

Arlaya just turned to him, softly stroking his damaged shoulders, "Of course I do."

"Can I come to you? I need you so much."

She just rolled on her back and held up her arms to him.

Next morning Arken came round before Arlaya had finished treating Nemroz's shoulders. "How are your wounds healing? It is a while since I treated them."

"Oh, they are healing fine now thanks."

"Are you eating breakfast today?"

"Yes please."

When Ker and Hella joined them, Ker still did not seem friendly to either Nemroz or Arken. When Arken asked if they were still preparing the field, Ker snapped, "You are misleading Nemroz."

Before Arken had time to answer, Nemroz said, "You are wrong there, it was me who asked Arken about his god. He is helping me. I think we should all learn about this god who loves all mankind."

No-one seemed to know how to answer him.

After breakfast Ker fetched his tools and set out for the field, so Nemroz and Arken fetched theirs and followed. For a while they all worked in silence, until Arken asked how Nemroz got on yesterday. Nemroz looked nervously at Ker.

"Don't worry, if Ker will not talk to us, just talk to me."

"I found what you said very interesting, but I am not sure about talking to your Lord."

"It will come with practice, and remember He is your Lord too now."

It was an uncomfortable day. They both at times tried to talk to Ker, but he did not respond. Late afternoon Nemroz and Arken took their tools and left. When they got back to the shelter the women were busy. They were pleased when they took little Roz and amused him by playing with him. Ker did not appear until the meal was ready.

Ker still did not have much to say, and he did not speak to Nemroz or Arken at all. Later Nemroz and Arken offered to fetch the food from the maids. The leading maid said, "Tell Ker there is a cow he can borrow for the time being, if he will come to the farm tomorrow."

When they got back and told the others, Ker said to Hella, "Come on we are going to bed."

Arlaya went to interrupt, but Arken said, "Leave it, we should all go to bed."

Next morning Roz was awake early, he crawled in between his parents. Nemroz stroked his now lustrous head of auburn hair, just like his mother's, sighing quietly, "I never thought I would be allowed to have the love of a beautiful women and that I would have the pleasure of a lovely little son." He added, "I hope when he is older, he will appreciate knowing his parents."

He thought Arlaya was still asleep until she wiped the tear from his eye, and she whispered, "I hope we make up for you not knowing yours."

"Oh, my darling I love you."

At breakfast Ker was reminded of the promise of the cow. It was decided that Ker, Hella and Arlaya would go to the farm and Nemroz and Arken would stay to look after Roz.

They were greeted by several of the farmhands saying,

"Pops and his brother Rutter have said you can borrow this cow. She has recently had a calf, so she should give milk for some time." As they did not have even the basic equipment, they borrowed a pail and a stool as well.

They were told they could borrow what else they needed, but that in time they would have to pay for them, or return them. They drove the cow and carried the pail and the stool back to the shelter.

The women were delighted. Though they did not have a shed for the cow, the field was large enough for a meadow. Now they would have enough milk to complete Roz's weaning. They had also been promised some sheep later in the year.

Milking had now become part of the women's routine. They had more than they needed as fresh milk, so they began making cheese. Soon when the vegetables had grown, they would have begun to become self-sufficient.

CHAPTER

6

The next morning when Nemroz woke, Arlaya and Roz were still asleep. Nemroz lay there thinking how different life was now to when he was in the temple. But he was concerned how things would work out. When they were offered this little farm, they were to have worked it between them and Ker. Now if Ker would no longer co-operate, what would happen? But he did not regret his commitment to Arken's god.

When Arlaya woke she found him in tears. "Darling, what is the matter? Yesterday you were so happy?"

"Now we would have milk for Polto."

"You still miss those priests, don't you?"

"I will always miss them, especially Darius."

"If you want to give some milk to Polto, why don't you take him an offering? Or don't you priests do that?"

"I am not sure Arken would agree with that."

"Why do you always do what Arken says these days?"

"You used to be interested in what Arken had to say."

"It is Arken's god who has come between you and Ker."

"I am worried about that. We were to have shared the farm and built the farmhouse between us."

"Then forget this foreign god."

"He is a god who loves us, he does not require us to sacrifice poor innocent girls, he sacrificed himself. How can you reject a god like that?"

"Oh Nemroz, I don't know what to do with you. Let's go to breakfast."

"Will you try to find out from Hella what is happening? Ker will not speak to me."

At breakfast Nemroz asked whether they were working in the field. But Ker still did not answer, so Arken just collected their tools and went to the field, Nemroz followed. Later Ker was furious because they had not helped him collect some equipment. At the evening meal Nemroz challenged Ker, "How can we know what is needed if you will not talk to us?"

Hella said, "Ker please, we cannot run the farm on our own. This was a wonderful opportunity."

"Well, they must forget this forgeign god then."

Then when no one challenged him, Arlaya joined in, "Why?"

When no one responded, she turned to Nemroz saying, "Please tell Ker what you told me this morning."

Nemroz hesitated, then said, "I could not reject Arken's god. He is a god who loves us. He is not like the god I was brought up to serve." Then his voice faded away, and he just added, "I love him."

He turned to Arken and said, "Can I talk to you?"

"Of course, come to my shelter."

Nemroz turned to Arlaya saying, "Sorry, I will see you later."

The two of them left. As they crawled into Arken's shelter Nemroz said, "It is so small. How do you manage?"

"It is only for me."

"We cannot even stand up. Can I hold you?"

Arken crawled in and held out his arms to Nemroz.

"I thought you did not agree with that."

"I must admit, when you embraced me the other day, I found it quite comforting."

Nemroz rushed to him and threw his arms round him. "How do you manage here all alone? I am so lucky, I have Arlaya and that is more than I ever though I could have. But I still miss Darius."

"Like you I have learnt control. It seems to me you still feel you should not have the love of a woman."

"I misunderstood you. But I did not come to talk about that. I am worried about the situation with Ker and the farm. If he will no longer co-operate. Where does that leave us?"

"I think when I first knew you, you would have taken control of the situation."

"I suppose you are right. Since the journey from Pop's farm, I am different. Please help me."

"We should pray. I want you to practice speaking to the Lord through your spirit. I would not ask that of any other new convert, but I believe you are special."

"You have too high an expectation of me."

"I do not think so. Please be patient and persistent."

They knelt together for some time. Then Arken realized Nemroz was quietly crying. "It is all right. It will come in time."Arken threw his arms round him.

"Thankyou, I have longed for you to do that. I promised I would never do anything you think is wrong, but I miss Darius so much."

"I am so sorry I was not able to prevent that. Please forgive me."

"I am sure it was not your fault. Please just be a friend to me."

"That would be wonderful. I chose this path. I am used to it, but it is very lonely."

"Oh, Arken I so misjudged you. Does your...our Lord speak to you?"

"Sometimes."

What does He say?"

"He reminds me there are many things I have not yet taught you, and that there are things I should do,"

"Such as?"

"The Lord told his first followers that there is something they should do in memory of Him."

"What is that?"

"It is hard, things are so different here… how can you understand, there is still so much I have not told you."

"I should go to Arlaya, she will wonder where I am. I will come to you again as soon as I can."

When Nemroz got back to their little space Arlaya was asleep. He slid in beside her. When she woke next morning, she was relieved to find Nemroz beside her. She threw her arms round him and he woke and gazed sleepily at her.

"Where did you get to?"

"I talked to Arken longer than I intended."

"Ker was furious, there was no one to go with him to fetch the food from the maids."

"If he wants to run the place without us, that is the kind of problem he will have to solve."

"Darling you will get us thrown out. Then where will we go?"

"We will tackle that if it happens."

"I am not happy about that, but it does sound more like the old you."

"Have you got any of the treatment for my shoulders left?"

"Yes, I made some the other day."

"Will you treat them please. Then can we have some breakfast?"

Arken joined them for breakfast, but there was no sign of Ker and Hella.

Arlaya was concerned. "Should I go and see if they are alright?"

"I am sure they will be down." Nemroz replied.

"But perhaps the baby is coming early. I must go and see." Without waiting for approval, she went to climb onto the cart.

She came hurrying down. Arken asked anxiously, "What's wrong?"

"Ker threw me out."

Nemroz leapt up to have it out with him, but Arken stopped him.

Arlaya said, "I am getting worried about all this. Can't you two put a stop to it?"

"What would you suggest?"

"Stop all this about this god of yours."

"If you understood, you would know we cannot do that."

Arlaya burst into tears, and Nemroz tried to comfort her.

But she sobbed, "Do not leave me here on my own."

Arken said, "I will fetch the tools, please brink little Roz, we will all go to the field together."

"But I must milk the cow first."

"That is alright. We will wait for you." Arken went with her and helped. While Nemroz stayed with Roz.

Then Arken carried the tools and Nemroz carried Roz. Arken and Nemroz spent the day preparing more ground, and Arlaya played with little Roz. He thought it was great having attention all day.

Late afternoon they returned to the shelter. They found Ker and Hella were nowhere to be seen. Arlaya prepared the food, and they ate their meal. They were getting worried when there was no sign of the others.

In the evening, when it was time to fetch the food from the maids,

Nemroz said, "We maybe some time, I am going to try to find out what is happening. Arken will you come with me, and Arlaya will you put Roz to bed and stay in the shelter? I will be back as soon as I can."

Nemroz left with Arken. They met with the maids as usual, but Nemroz asked whether any of the maids had seen Ker and Hella.

One of them said, "They are eating in the farmhand's hall."

So, they left the food where it was, and the maid took Nemroz and Arken to the farmhand's hall.

They entered the hall, and sure enough Ker and Hella were there eating with the farmhands. Arken approached him and knelt beside him saying, "Sir, we need to know whether you intend to continue to work on our little farm."

"It is my farm!"

"When we arrived, Rutter, who owns this farm, loaned that area to be worked by Nemroz, you and myself."

Ker just demanded, "Throw them out!"

Two of the farmhands carried Arken, still in a kneeling position and threw him at Nemroz. They staggered into the maid's arms.

"Can you take us to Rutter?"

"What now?"

"Yes now."

One of the maids turned and Nemroz and Arken followed her straight to the farmhouse.

"You wait there, I will see whether Rutter will see you." Soon she returned saying, "Follow me."

They had never been in Rutter's farmhouse before, it seemed much grander than Pops's had been. The maid opened a door saying, "In here please."

Rutter was sitting on a large couch. Nemroz and Arken stood before him and politely bowed their heads. Nemroz began, "We are very grateful for your generous loan of the area by the lower stream."

"Yes, yes." Rutter interrupted impatiently.

"But we have a problem."

"What is the matter with it?"

"There is nothing the matter with the farm sir. The problem is with Ker."

"Well tell him to come and see me."

"He will not work with us. He will not even talk to us."

"Tell him to come here."

"When we tried to approach him, he threw us out of the servants' hall."

"He has no right to do things like that. He is not even family; he is only a servant." Rutter called, and a servant entered the room. "Go to the servants' hall and fetch Ker straight away."

"Yes sir."

"What have you done to course this?"

Arken replied, "We have always worked hard sir, and done our best to co-operate. As I understand, the arrangement was for us to work the farm between us."

Rutter muttered under his breath, "I see what my brother means, these priests are trouble."

Soon the servant returned dragging Ker behind him.

"You wimp! Did you go telling tales?"

Rutter was disgusted. "Enough of that. What is this all about?"

"I am not working with that!"

"Why not? I thought it was a good opportunity. You will not get another opportunity like that."

"I agree sir, all ruined by those two."

"Why, what have they done?"

"They worship foreign gods and refuse to work."

"Rutter sir, please help me. I am so grateful for this opportunity; all I want is to work. I have always worked hard, whether it was for your brother or pulling the cart. Is there no one else who would be prepared to work with me?"

"I know my brother does not like you, but everyone says you work hard. I think you Ker and your wife should return to your duties on the farm. I am sure there are others who would like the opportunity of a farm of their own. Even if it is to be shared with two ex-priests. Is your wife at the farm?"

"Yes sir."

"Then fetch her and return to the servants' quarters.

"Ker snarled at Nemroz, "I will get you for this."

Then Rutter said to Nemroz, "Return to the new farm. Come and see me tomorrow."

"Yes sir. Thankyou sir." They all left.

Nemroz and Arken fetched the food on the way back.

Arken said, "I should have said I would leave; all this is my fault."

Nemroz replied, "No, please don't do that. I need you as a friend, and there is a lot more I still need to learn."

Arken muttered under his breath, "You are amazing."

By the time they got back to the shelter it was late, and Arlaya was already in bed. Nemroz slipped in beside her. She asked, "Is that you Nemroz?"

"Yes darling, you go to sleep, I will tell you all about it tomorrow." He put his arms round her and they both went to sleep.

Next morning, he told her, Ker and Hella were not coming back. And Arlaya was most alarmed.

"How will we manage? We cannot manage a farm on our own."

"We saw Rutter last night. He was kinder than I expected. He said he will find someone else to share the farm with us. I am to go back to him today, with Arken, to discuss the future."

"Why would he do that?"

"I told you Arken's god would look after us."

"It is because of his god that we are in this mess."

"It will be alright, you will see."

After breakfast he asked, "Can you manage the milking? If you can't manage the pail, leave it. We will see to it when we get back. If it gets spilt, it won't matter. We have enough for now."

"Please don't leave me."

"We need to get this sorted."

Arken interrupted, "Would it be better if I stay with Arlaya?"

"If you would both be happier, I will go alone."

CHAPTER

7

Nemroz set out for the main farm. He hesitated at the farmhouse door. Hella came rushing up to him, "Nemroz please help me. Ker's stupidity has lost us the farm. He blames you."

"Do you think it is my fault?"

"No not really, I do not think you have done anything wrong."

"What do you think I can do for you?"

"Please take me in."

"I can't do that; I have a wife."

"Arken doesn't."

"I don't think Arken will take a wife."

"Because of his god I suppose. That is the cause of all this in the first place."

"I don't think that is fair. Anyway, I am to see Rutter now. I mustn't keep him waiting."

"Can I come too?"

"If he sees you, it will be with Ker."

"Nemroz I am scared."

"Wait here, I will tell you later what is said." Then he knocked at the door.

A servant came to the door. "Rutter is expecting me." Nemroz said, trying hard to sound confident.

"Wait there, I will see if he is ready for you." He soon returned, "Please come in."

Nemroz was a little surprise at the genteel greeting in a farmer's house. He followed the servant into the room he had entered yesterday. Rutter was waiting for him.

"Now about what happened yesterday. How are you and your wife getting on with the farm, and where is the other one?"

"Arken is staying to look after my wife."

"Do you trust this priest with your wife?" Rutter interrupted.

"Yes sir. May I say first how grateful we are for your generosity."

"Yes, yes, you will have to pay for it all when the farm is up and running."

"I am hoping we will soon be independent. We have part of the small field with vegetables growing, and with the milk from the cow we are making cheese."

"Do you think that is independence?"

"That is all we had at your brother's farm."

"He said things were bad, but I did not think they were as bad as that. Would you be able to run the farm between the three of you?"

"I am afraid not sir. My friend and I were brought up as priests, so we know little of farming. My wife knows more, but she knows little of the work the men did."

"I see why you were worried about losing Ker. I am sure there are others who would be pleased to take Ker's place. But how I will decide who is suitable and deserving is another matter."

Nemroz was more amazed than ever. Wanting to say, 'are we deserving,' but thought better of it.

"Will you be able to manage for a few days?"

"I am sure we will sir. May I ask a favour?"

"Yes, yes, what?"

"May Hella join us?"

"I have withdrawn Ker from your part of the farm, surely Hella will be with her husband."

"She did not want to leave our part of the farm. She says she would rather be with us."

"Have you asked her?"

"She came to me this morning."

"Where?"

"Outside your farmhouse sir."

"Is she still there?"

"I think so."

"Go and get her."

Nemroz went straight outside to see whether Hella was still there, he asked her to see Rutter.

"Well, Nemroz told me you want to return to the farm by the lower stream."

"With your permission sir. It was very generous of you. It was an opportunity of a lifetime. My husband was very foolish to turn it down."

"I would agree with that. But are you willing to leave your husband?"

"I would rather live with Nemroz and Arken than a fool."

"I will risk it, but if there is any trouble you must leave. Now, do you still need the food the maids bring you?"

"If you would be so kind. The vegetables are still growing, and the cheese will not be ready for a while yet."

"Alright, I will send a message via the maids when I have made a decision on a replacement for your husband. Now go and get some work done both of you."

When they got back, Arlaya rushed to greet them, throwing her arms round Hella, she cried, "I thought you weren't coming back."

Ker isn't, but all being well I am."

Nemroz asked, "Where is Arken?"

"He went to the field."

"You women get on with the women's work. I will go to the field." He left the women embracing.

When he reached the field Arken came and embraced him too, saying, "I may have introduced you to my God, but you have converted me to greeting you like this, I do not know what my people would think of it."

"I don't care, I love it."

They worked together for the rest of the day. In the evening they went to fetch the supplies as usual.

The next day when they went to fetch the supplies, the head maid informed them that Rutter wanted to see them in the morning.

On the way back Arken said, "Tomorrow is the Lord's Day."

"Well surely going to see Rutter is not work."

"But it isn't worshipping the Lord."

"I am prepared to follow what you say, but there are limits."

"I have been pleased with your progress. You go alone to see Rutter. But there were some important things I hoped to teach you tomorrow."

"When I get back, I will come to you tonight."

"What about Arlaya?"

"She has Hella to keep her company."

When they got back Nemroz explained, "I need some time with Arken. Will you be alright with Hella?"

Nemroz and Arken went to Arken's little shelter. "Now what is it you need to tell me?"

"The Lord has been reminding me of an important process the early followers were taught to do, which we should continue. Things are very different here, so it is not easy. The early followers would have understood more of what He was doing. He took bread and wine. He broke the bread, saying, "This is my body broken for you." And He took the wine saying, "This is the new covenant in my blood, which is shed for you." We are to do this to remind us of His sacrifice for us. When we were at Pop's farm that wasn't possible, we did not have bread or wine."

Nemroz replied, "Not much of that makes much sense to me."

"I realize that. But if we obey, it shows we remember the great sacrifice the Lord made for us. You can learn about the details as we go along."

"I do appreciate what he has done for us, but how can we obey without bread and wine?"

"You can help me think about that. You should return to Arlaya now."

"Can I give you a hug?"

Arken looked at him and smiled. Nemroz gave him a hug and left.

Next morning after breakfast Nemroz said to Arken, "You go to your Lord, I will see you later." And he left for the farmhouse. Nemroz knocked on the door, and was shown into see Rutter.

"Good morning sir." Nemroz said, with a slight bow.

"I have someone for you to meet. His name is Garvon and his wife's is Pretta. They are coming to help teach you how to run a farm."

"You are very kind sir. I hope we will make a success of it for you."

"How you sort out who stays with whom is up to you. I am not sure I have the resources for you to build a farmhouse. Take them with you now."

The three of them thanked Rutter again and left. While walking back to the shelter Nemroz explained, "Our home is very poor. It is made from a cart. We live below the cart, and Ker and Hella lived above. But Hella still lives there above us. If you take their quarters, I do not know where Hella will stay."

When they got back, they all introduced themselves, only Arken was missing, he was in his little shelter.

Hella suggested, "Could we build a shelter in the other half of the cart? Something like Arken's."

"Who is Arken?" asked Garvon.

"Arken is my friend. He is busy today. We will meet him later."

Hella took Garvon to see Arken's shelter. Then the women went collecting materials for the thatch, and Nemroz and Garvon took the axe to find good uprights for the shelter and suitable supports for the thatch. They all worked hard all day and the shelter was built. When Arken joined them later, Hella was keen to show him what they had built. There was not yet a cover over the entrance, otherwise it was finished.

The next day the three men went working in the field, and the three women milked the cow, and things like making the cheese. Everyone seemed to be getting on well with each other.

After the evening meal, Nemroz said to Arken, "Will you help me fetch the food from the maids?"

On the way Nemroz said, "I have been thinking about what you said about remembering the Lord. We had a ritual meal in the temple. We had access to wine then. There were three symbols. There was milk, which was Farago's provision, wine, which was sanctification, and water, which was suffering. You said in the sample prayer that, 'our daily bread' was God's provision for us. Would milk be the same as bread?"

"I am sure you are trying to help, but there is much you still do not understand. Come to my shelter when we get back."

They brought the food to the women and Nemroz apologised he needed to talk to Arken. They left and settled in the shelter.

"I have not been able to explain yet about the times and situation when the Lord lived on this earth. The bread in question was a symbol of His body which was to be broken for them. I realize you did not understand. You see why we could not use milk."

"I did not realize. We need something we can break."

"I have never taught anyone who appreciates things as you do."

"My priest's training did not help with farming. But I understand things like that."

"I am lucky to have a friend like you. Can I explain the significance of the wine?"

"If you would."

"The wine represents the Lord's blood that was poured out to seal the new covenant (agreement) between God and mankind."

"Does that have to be wine?"

"It was wine originally. I will have to talk to the Lord about that. You try talking to Him about it yourself. I will speak to you about it again soon."

Nemroz gave him a hug, then returned to Arlaya.

The next few days work continued as before, interrupted only occasionally by rain, as the wet season was approaching. Then it was the next seventh day. This time having been forewarned, Garvon was not annoyed. He was curious, so was invited to join them. Arken started by explaining they were asking their God to join them. Then having prayed he said, "Please join me in my shelter later and I will start from the beginning for you. For now, I need to talk to Nemroz," he asked, "What thoughts have you had about the bread and wine?"

"Sometimes we have bread. I have brought some from the other day. Will that be acceptable? Wine is made from water. Until we have means for making wine, would water do?"

"I am sure that the Lord will appreciate that you are trying hard. I am sure He will accept your efforts. Did you bring these things with you?"

"Yes, they are here."

"I do not expect you to learn everything at once. I will talk us through the service and, if Garvon can just watch for now."

After celebrating communion, Arken said to Garvon, "Would you like to come to my shelter, I will start to explain what this is all about. Would you like to come and help Nemroz?"

"I will go to see Arlaya, to see whether she can help with something to replace bread, if that is alright."

A shelter had been made for the cheese making. The three women were working in there. Little Roz saw Nemroz coming and came to greet him. Nemroz picked him up and swung him round. Roz giggled. Nemroz asked if Arlaya would come and talk to him. The three of them went into their home under the cart.

"Will you help us?"

"Us! Is that you and Arken?"

"Do you mind that?"

"This Arken causes trouble."

"I do not understand. You used to be interested in what Arken teaches."

"Only because you wanted me to. But he caused trouble and my friend lost her husband."

"I cannot see that was Arken's fault, but can you not just help me?"

"What do you want me to do?"

"We need bread. There is very seldom bread in the food we eat. Would you be able to make something like bread from say, vegetables?"

"Is the food we provide not good enough for you?"

"If you would come to Arken with me, you could learn what it is for."

"Find someone else to teach your strange ideas. I am going back to help the others. Come on Roz."

Feeling upset and hurt Nemroz sat wondering what else he could do. Wanting to follow Arken's ideas he did not think he should work in the field, so he went to Arken's shelter.

"Is there room for me in there?" he called.

"We can make room." Arken replied. Nemroz turned to Garvon and said, "Are you understanding what Arken is teaching?"

"It all seems very strange, but I suppose I will learn in time."

"Sorry to interrupt, but would cheese be any good when we have no bread? You can break cheese."

"My dear friend, I don't know anyone like you."

"Is there anything I can help with?"

They continued with teaching for the rest of the day.

When it was getting near time for the evening meal, Garvon and Arken went to join the women. But Nemroz went to spend a little time with Darius and Polto.

As Arken approached Hella ran to meet him. "Where have you been all day?"

"We have been with my Lord. The seventh day is the Lord's Day."

"Next time can I come too? I want to learn about your Lord."

"We would be pleased for you to join us."

"Can I come to your shelter?"

"I think it would be best if you wait until we are all together next time."

By then Nemroz was in earshot, and he hurried to his friend's side. "I think that would be best."

Arken gave Nemroz a smile and whispered, "Can I see you later?"

After the meal Nemroz asked Arken to come with him to collect the supplies. On the way he said, "What is the matter my friend?"

"I do still appreciate you addressing me like that."

"Are you going to tell me what is wrong?"

"I would rather you came to my shelter when we get back."

So, they walked on in silence. Then when they got back, they went to the shelter.

"I think you are the only one who can understand my problem."

"Why what is wrong?"

"Hella is paying me more and more attention. Today she asked to come to my shelter."

"Is that so wrong?"

"Hella has a husband, and I am a priest. We should return to the others."

"You are in trouble. What is the matter?"

"I am a priest; I have pledged not to take a wife."

Nemroz turned away. The significance hit him. "I should not have a wife. But I never pledged that, it was what was expected of me. I never chose to be a priest. I was donated to the priesthood when I was a baby."

"I am sorry, you understood me more than I understood you. Forgive me."

"But I still think I should not have taken a wife." Nemroz ran from the shelter and ran to the grave.

Next morning when Arken went to breakfast, he found Arlaya sobbing that Nemroz had not come in all night. And he went looking for him. He found him on the grave, and was shocked to find he had been there all night. Arken knelt beside him saying, "I did not mean to criticize you, I only thought you would understand."

Nemroz sobbed, "Polto was right, I should never have taken a wife."

"Come on your wife is lovely and she is worried about you." He took Nemroz by the hand. And he allowed himself to be led to breakfast.

Everyone thought Nemroz had got over it, he went to the field and worked all day. But that night he woke with the nightmare again. Arlaya tried to calm him. But his screaming woke Roz.

Nemroz said, "You go to see to Roz, I cannot have my problems disturbing the little one."

Poor Arlaya was torn in two as Nemroz rushed out.

The next night he said, "I must not sleep here, I will wake you and little Roz, that is not fair."

"Darling where will you go?"

"I will be alright. Do not follow me. You look after the little one."

Each night he spent prostrated on the grave. He was tearing himself apart. Neither Arlaya nor Arken could help him.

This went on for several nights. Then one night, no one realized Nemroz had taken one of Arlaya's sharp cooking knives with him. He calmly removed his clothes, folded them and lay them by the hedge. He stood over the grave, and with one swift blow, he executed the Farago priest's punishment on himself. Then collapsed face down on the grave.

When Nemroz did not come to breakfast next day, Arken went looking for him. He found him motionless, naked, face down on the grave. When he rolled him over, he was horrified at the sight before him. He rushed back to the others, ashen faced and trembling. Garvon asked, "What is the matter?"

Arken stuttered, "Nemroz has killed himself!"

Arlaya guessed where he was, and rushed to be by his side. Arken tried to stop her, but she was gone. As she approached the grave she stopped, stunned by what she saw. Arken had run after her, and she collapsed into his arms. "Come you should not have seen this."

She turned to him and said, "No, I must go to him." As she knelt by his side, she sobbed, "When we were first married, he said, no one succeeded him as High Priest, so he should exercise the Farago priest's punishment on himself. But I never thought he would do it."

Arlaya insisted the grave was to be opened, and Nemroz was to be laid with his friends. He was to be laid above them face down. Arlaya insisted in life she had always had to share him with his priests. He is to lie with them in death. And in view of what had happened, he is to be face down and naked.

Arken protested saying, "This is not right, Nemroz is a Christian now."

Arlaya insisted, "He is my husband, it is not for you to say what happens to him."

They compromised; Arken made a headstone with all three names on to replace the cairns.

CHAPTER

Arken moved in with Arlaya. He looked after her and little Roz for the rest of his life, but he never lay with her. He always said if she wanted to remarry, he would move out. But Arlaya always insisted no one could ever replace Nemroz. After Hella's baby was born she returned to Ker. In time Garvon, Pretta and Arlaya all converted to Arken's beliefs. But Nemroz was always greatly missed. Arken had done his best. But had Nemroz truly understood the meaning of repentance, that it is not just that you are sorry. But that it is a complete turn around and surrendering one's life to God. He may have realized that he was forgiven for all that had gone before in his life, and that the Farago punishment was no longer required.

Nemroz never intended to end his life. But what he did caused him to bleed to death. Pain ended and all went black. He had no idea how long this empty peace lasted.

When Nemroz chose to believe in Arken's creator God and accepted what He had done for him, a new spirit was born in him. That spirit would live forever.

But because of what had happened to him, his situation was rather different to that of his friends. When Nemroz became aware that the nothingness had ended, he found he was still in the world. But he was different. He realized that when he tried to take hold of something with, what he thought was his hand, it passed straight through it.

And when he tried to speak to someone they did not seem to be able to hear him. He was beginning to feel very isolated and helpless. And more and more miserable.

When he found there seemed to be no way out of his situation, he began to try all sorts of ways to cope. There were some advantages, he did not get hungry or thirsty, and he did not need to worry about things like clothes.

Gradually he learnt to use his mind, (which very much still worked), to convey his thoughts to others. (It worked with some people, but not with others.) But sadly most of the people he reached thought he was just their imagination. There were a few rare occasions when somebody realized someone or something was trying to communicate with them. Nemroz was relieved and delighted. But unfortunately, because of the limitations of his situation it made life very difficult, and the contact never lasted very long.

It was a strange time for Nemroz, he did not seem to be in the world for long each time. It was as though he went back to sleep. Each time he reawakened, he was in a different time and place.

Then one time when he woke, he tried yet again. This time he made contact with someone who seemed interested in who he was, and what had happened to him. He was afraid at first it would not last, and it would end as it had done before. But this time things seemed to be much more successful.

He found that the world now seemed much more complicated than he had known before, and there was much more to learn.

As he grew more confident with his new contact, he began to take an interest in the kind of things she was doing, and later began to be involved with the things she was involved with. She had a strange machine, when she pressed various buttons etc. it seemed to talk. Often, they listened together to the things it had to say.

Sometimes it told them what was happening in other parts of the world. Sometimes she said they were just stories someone had made up. And sometimes people were talking about the Lord Jesus. Nemroz was amazed, he asked whether that was the same Lord Jesus that

Arken had taught him about. When he was told that it was, more and more he asked to listen to the voice talking about the Lord Jesus. They listened to sermons, programmes and books that read themselves. He was fascinated to learn more than Arken had ever taught him.

CHAPTER

By studying with his new contact, Nemroz began to learn many more things about God, His people and His intentions for the world He had once intended to share with mankind. These are a few of the things they learnt. That this special God chose for Himself a special people who were supposed to worship only Him. But that they often failed. He learnt many stories about that nation. He learnt many traditions that this people followed and the symbolic meaning of these traditions. Like the time when that nation was rescued from slavery in Egypt by their God. He did many things to the Egyptians to make them let God's people go, (these people were called the Israelites, nowadays they are called the Jews). Finally, He said if their leader did not let the Israelites go, He would kill all their firstborn. The Egyptian leader still refused to let the Israelites go, so God did kill all the firstborn. So that all the Israelite families were spared they were to mark their door surrounds with blood. Not one of their firstborn died. This event was commemorated every year by all Israelite families from that day to this. This commemoration is called 'the Passover'. Exodus Chapters 5-12.

There were many other stories from Hebrew history where God foretold, often symbolically, the things He intended to do. Some of these have not happened yet, though many have.

He demonstrated that it would be possible to substitute one life for another, and because it would be a long time (by mankind's time scale) for this to take place the way God had planned, God showed them by introducing the system of animal sacrifice. For many centuries the Israelite people followed the practise of animal sacrifice, thinking that the death of the animal would cover their sin. Probably no-one in heaven or on earth knew the significance of what they were doing.

The special animal sacrifice that accompanied the Passover meal was a special lamb. There were very special regulations that applied to that lamb. The Passover is still a special meal the Jewish families have together. All the elements of the meal are symbolic. All the members of the families share these elements, retelling the story of God rescuing their ancestors from Egypt. One of these elements is a cup of wine they call the 'cup of redemption'. The significance of this was not known by anyone until Jesus celebrated the Passover meal with His followers. (Christians call this 'The Last Supper').

When Jesus had finished the meal, He took this cup and announced that it represented His blood, that was to be shed to seal the 'New Covenant' between God and mankind.

The Passover Lamb was a depiction of Jesus Himself. The crucifixion of Jesus was the sacrifice of the true and final Passover Lamb. Until that point the sin of mankind had come between God and His special creation. What Jesus achieved was the major step in God's plan to return His world to the way He originally intended it to be. By accepting that Jesus had paid the price we should have paid, God now accepted us as the creation we should have been.

When God was teaching His people on the journey from Egypt. He demonstrated His presence with them in several ways. One was to have them create a special place which demonstrated His awesome holiness had to be separated from the sin of man. He had instructed them to make the tabernacle (a mobile temple they carried with them through the desert). In it was a special area called 'the holy of holies', which was separated from the main area by a great curtain. In the 'holy of holies' was an ark, (an amazing chest, covered with gold inside and out), in which were held the tablets of stone on which the instructions He had given the Israelites were kept. This was to represent God's presence.

When at last the Israelites had a permanent homeland, a wonderful stone structure replaced the tabernacle. There were many courtyards where various people were allowed to go. In the central area, only the priests were allowed to go. The holy of holies was housed in the middle of that. The ark and the presence of God was divided even from the priests by the great curtain.

At the moment when the sacrifice the Lord Jesus made was achieved, that great curtain was torn from TOP to BOTTOM. Signifying that there was now access for the human race to God through Jesus Christ.

Before God created mankind, He created another form of creation. (the spiritual realm). We refer to the creatures in that realm as angels. For a very long time they worked with God as He intended. There were many ranks of angels; it all worked harmoniously, with all the angels working together, with God as their supreme leader. But when God said He was going to create another level of creation to work with Him in His new world He had created, some of the angels rebelled against that idea. One of the leading angels did his best to dissuade God from His idea. But God is the supreme power, and no-one can overpower Him.

God created mankind and placed them on His new world. The leading angel and many others who agreed with him did their best to prove God wrong. God had intended His new creation to co-operate with Him. The rebellious angels tempted the humans to go their own way. Unfortunately, they succeeded, for the time being. God was furious with the rebellious angels. He threw them out of heaven, never allowing them to return.

Realizing that they had failed, and that they had lost their life in their ideal realm, they took it out on mankind.

At the fall (mankind's first disobedience), God said Adam and Eve, (the first couple), would die that day. Their physical body did not die straight away. Though their bodies started dying from then on. But their spiritual life (the part of them that was united with God) did. God could not be united with sin.

Only God knew what He was going to do to rectify the situation. God knew the only sacrificial substitute death would be the death of a perfect life. There was no-one on earth who is not tainted by sin. So, God came to earth Himself. He experienced everything that is involved in human life, from being born, all the temptations in life, and death. Even separation (in a sense from Himself) in hell. And having achieved that, without failing in one detail, the price was paid.

When God first created man to share His world with Him, He knew just how He wanted things to be. Even though we spoiled that plan, God never changes His mind. Neither these angels nor mankind could ever change what God chose to do. How ever long it would take, He would have the world the way He intended in the end. When God showed the first stage of His plan, the bad angels realized that mankind had a way to be forgiven and return to God's plan. But when they realized that did not include them, they were even more furious and resentful towards mankind. They continued to try to destroy mankind and get as many as they could to rebel against God. Or if they could not do that, they tried to stop them from getting to know God, or stop them doing what God wanted them to do.

One of the elements of God's plan was that the next stage would not take place until everyone in the world had heard about God. One of the rebellious angels' tactics was to do their best to impede that process. As one of the preachers put it, "Keep kicking the can down the road." But no-one has the power to thwart God.

Having achieved the sacrificial death that paid the price for sin, Jesus did not stay dead. On the third day He rose from the dead. Proving who was, and that if we live in Him and Him in us, we too will rise from the dead. So that we will live forever in union with God as He originally intended.

There is lots of debate about these details. Nemroz admits he is no expert, and would advise you to continue with research for yourself. There is a lot of information on channels like YouTube. But be careful it is from reliable preachers like Dr. Charles Stanley and Stephen

Meyer. Some of the books he listened to are, 'God in Sandals', 'The Unseen Realm' and 'Beyond Mere Belief".

Another problem that was probably started by the bad angels, is the distorted picture of hell. The best book Nemroz recommends is 'The Skeletons in God's Closet' by Joshua Ryan Butler